Dear Parent:
Your child's love of reading starts here!

Every child learns to read in a different way and at his or her own speed. You can help your young reader improve and become more confident by encouraging his or her own interests and abilities. You can also guide your child's spiritual development by reading stories with biblical values and Bible stories, like I Can Read! books published by Zonderkidz. From books your child reads with you to the first books he or she reads alone, there are I Can Read! books for every stage of reading:

 My First
SHARED READING
Basic language, word repetition, and whimsical illustrations, ideal for sharing with your emergent reader.

 1
BEGINNING READING
Short sentences, familiar words, and simple concepts for children eager to read on their own.

 2
READING WITH HELP
Engaging stories, longer sentences, and language play for developing readers.

 3
READING ALONE
Complex plots, challenging vocabulary, and high-interest topics for the independent reader.

 4
ADVANCED READING
Short paragraphs, chapters, and exciting themes for the perfect bridge to chapter books.

I Can Read! books have introduced children to the joy of reading since 1957. Featuring award-winning authors and illustrators and a fabulous cast of beloved characters, I Can Read! books set the standard for beginning readers.

A lifetime of discovery begins with the magical words **"I Can Read!"**

Visit www.icanread.com for information on enriching your child's reading experience.
Visit www.zonderkidz.com for more Zonderkidz I Can Read! titles.

Then you will understand what is right
and just and fair—every good path.
—Proverbs 2:9

ZONDERKIDZ

The Fairest Town in the West
Copyright © 2011 Big Idea Entertainment, LLC. VEGGIETALES®, character
names, likenesses and other indicia are trademarks of and copyrighted by Big Idea
Entertainment, LLC. All rights reserved.
Illustrations © 2011 by Big Idea Entertainment, Inc.

Requests for information should be addressed to:
Zonderkidz, Grand Rapids, Michigan 49530

ISBN 978-0-310-72729-3

Editor: Mary Hassinger
Art direction: Karen Poth
Cover design: Karen Poth
Interior design: Ron Eddy

Printed in China

12 13 14 15 16 /DSC/ 21 20 19 18 17 16 15 14 13 12 11 10 9 8 7 6 5 4 3 2

ZONDERkidz

I Can Read!

BEGINNING READING 1

The Fairest Town in the West

story by Karen Poth

Welcome to Dodge Ball City,

the fairest town in the west!

This is Sheriff Bob

and his deputy, Larry.

It is their job to keep the city peaceful

and the Dodge Ball games orderly!

On most days, their job is really fun!

They stop in at the

Rootin' Tootin' Pizza Place.

Then they go see their pals

at the Okie Dokie Corral.

At high noon, Bob and Larry have

a burger at Cow Patty's Cafe.

At two o'clock,

they have target practice

to get ready for the next big game.

They end their day by reading a bedtime
story to the town's one prisoner.
Bob and Larry love their job!

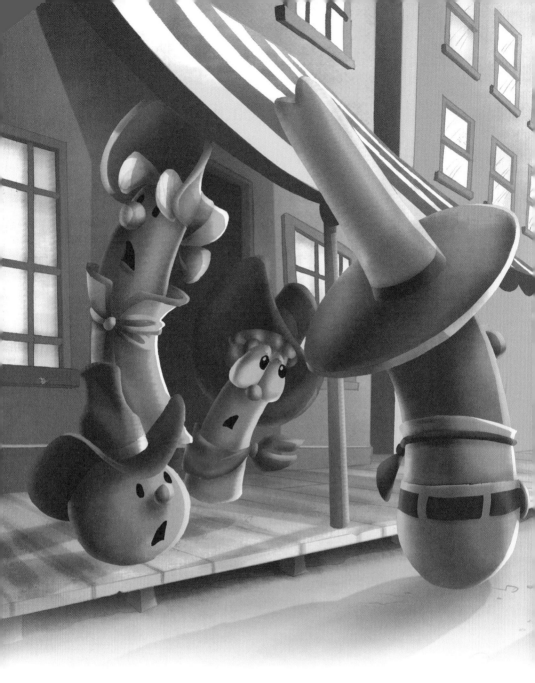

But one day Bob and Larry's job
got a lot harder.

The Ratt Scallion Gang

came to town.

Those Ratt Scallions just
didn't know how to behave!
They said mean things to EVERYONE.

They stole from the people in town.

And worst of all … they cheated!

Soon the whole town was acting this way.

Everyone was cheating.

Everyone was being mean to one another.

Something had to be done!

Dodge Ball City might stop being

the fairest town in the west!

Sheriff Bob got the town together.

He read the rules from the

Cowboy Code of the West.

"Page one," Bob read.

"A cowboy should always treat others
the way he wants to be treated!"

As Bob read the rules,

everyone started to remember

why their town was so special.

They decided

the rules made

a lot of sense!

"Play fair.

Always take turns.

Play by the rules.

"If you cheat all the time,

nobody will play with you!"

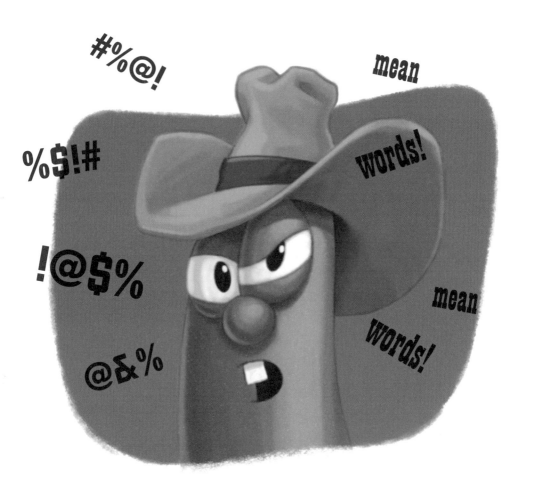

"Use nice words.

"If you say mean words
nobody will want
to talk to you!"

"Help your neighbor.

"If you're a stinker and don't help your neighbor, Sheriff Bob may put you in jail!"

"So what's it going to be, boys?"

Sheriff Bob asked the Ratt Scallions.

"Can we buy you a root beer, Sheriff?" said one of the Ratt Scallions with a smile.

Bob, Larry, and the Ratt Scallions
went to the Rootin' Tootin' Pizza Place.
They had a lot of fun!

Then they all played a game

of horseshoes … by the rules!

Deputy Larry won fair and square!

Appoint judges and officials for each of
your tribes in every town the LORD your
God is giving you, and they shall judge
the people fairly.

—Deuteronomy 16:18